Loves Flustering Glance

The Opening Chapters

A collection of short stories,
Written by J.E.M.

 www.trafford.com

North America & international
toll-free: 1 888 232 4444 (USA & Canada)
phone: 250 383 6864 ♦ fax: 812 355 4082

Contents

Flitting Thought

She walked across the busy road, evading the heavy traffic. Her skirt soaring through her inadequate movement. Issuing a supple glimpse of stocking lace, high on her elongated legs. She walked alone. Standing out, against the many pedestrians, that engaged with the tedious task of excursion. Her perky breasts, protruding through her silky blouse. Her clear, cream complexion, shimmering with the gentle glow of the evening sun. She was a vision. A picture to behold. She grabbed his attention and held it. He became a prisoner to his beating heart, hoping that probation would release his frozen posture on bail. He stood immobile. Unable to breathe, as he watched her shapely body, weaver elegantly towards him.

The day was hot, full of dust and fumes.
Elevating the angelic vision, further to the
heaven of his mind. His dispersion glands
opened. Shuddering. Releasing an untimely
drop. Sending momentary stimulant of
ecstasy through the cells of his susceptible
psyche. Unable to grapple with his mind, from
the hallucination of her. He licked his drying
lips. Opened his shirt, aiding his breathless
breathing. Time fragmented. Seeming to stop.
His quaint imagination, placed them alone.
Lifting them from the exposed, to seclusion.
She was his for that moment. Acquainting
her pose of lust, for his pleasure. He caressed
her sexual form! Tainting the proposition of
his mind, with a more exhibited aspiration.
Tasting her! Touching the sweet vigilance

in her descending elixir. Time ascended.

Becoming lost to his engaged deliberation. It

became too late to convey his appropriate wish.

She had walked by. She was gone . . . .

First
instinct

Relaxed; serene within the comfort of a scented lounge suite. She viewed him passing by. His grace. His posture. The whimsical nod, while in conversation. Marking his brow with a sexual, but knowledgeable frown; gathered her curiosity. His distant egotistical charisma, consumed; destroying her sureties. Echoed her yearning to glance exclusively in his direction. To her; there was no other male within that crowded room. No man, that could step in his shoes for her perceptive desire. Their eyes met. Exhilarating the moment. His flitting glare, conveyed shivers up her spine, as her love sick heart palpitated triple time. Embarrassment struck its despondent cord. She hastily turned. Was she found spying? She became timid, within the obscurely lit space. Tamed through shy naivety. Her spirit weakened by his powerful presence, becoming unsure of her projected aspiration. She had no reason obstructing her wants. No need to stifle her need, but her anchoring restraint withdrew her from the competitive issue to grasp for his companionship. She felt isolated. Why did this immense feeling happen to her? Confused within mixed emotions. Imagination became her soul mate, asking her to have a drink. Lifting her away from torment, landing her on the plane of serenity. In her wondrous mind, she sat thigh to thigh, allowing his manly embrace, instigate joyous laughter. Reality tapped on her shoulder. Awaking her from mad obscurity. She looked up. Bewilderment set the stage. It was her fantasy.

The gentleman of her lust, delivering her a dream. The first dream of many, she had created about him . . . .

What's the probability?

Bored of the consistent forum. The same tiresome weekend night out with the boys. Solitude played its remote rhythms within his despairing head. He searched the club for his prey. A victim of his depraved affection. The echoing memento searching for a different passion. A new outlet for his charms. A new means for adoration, when he glimpsed her enter from the corner of his eye. Clothed in label, she became a vision of is memoirs. Captivating the void density in his heart. He felt alive, alert. Frivolous in his heart and mind. Their eyes briefly met. He felt caught within a mendacious situation. Fatuous towards his announced desires of that night. Was it her? The one that halted his steps. Reintroducing the first impious instinct, that sent his mind back flipping to a new millennium. He hid away, masking the anxiety of his thoughts. Afraid to be found in vulnerability. But her entertaining lips, enthralled his kiss. The luscious depths in her eyes, ignited his craze. Her desirable physic, brought his obsession. Her slow sensual movement, lifted his moral. The intentional festivity for that night, vanished. Replaced, with a more softened eventful affair. Haste wanted the driving seat of his desire, urging his fatuous unknown hand to grasp the moment; while trepidation restrained this impetuous move. Suspending the ominous event for a more apt point in time. Pacifying; gathering his smooth ignition, to woo his candid lady. He voluntarily became communicative within the circulating guests, as he remained drawn towards her magnetic aura. Glancing prominently towards her direction, he finally step to the bar. Unable to contain himself, he ordered drinks, hoping to break the air of mystery . . . .

A
conversation
of sorts!!

Breathless at the mere sight of his presence, beside her. Clutching two alcoholic beverages for them to drink, subtracted the frigidity in the atmosphere. Barring the repulsive inclination of rejection from bounding lips. He introduced himself. His voice deep manly, robust. He became a new acquaintance to her yearning heart. She smirked at the quaint appraisal in their correlation; inhabited within her deviant thoughts. She was aiming to approach him, for what was in her mind. Musing each explicit second. Even considered making that move, after speculating, whether she was his type; and now she knew. Butterflies fluttered their quaking wings, tickling her inner soul. Flattering her spirit, with the anchoring hold of his admiration.

She watched him sit beside her, taking a long gapping sip of his drink. Lost in ore, the words escaped her thoughts. His masculine torso, rupturing through his loosely fitted shirt. His distinguished features enthralled her fem pleasure. Emptying her of solemn regrets. Was he the man for her? She hoped he was. The question repeated through her mind. A simple job. An easy test, became her responsibility. Treachery was her master. Her determination to uncover fraudulence in his performance, terminated the joyous affection she felt for him inside. It was to be her saviour. The deception of all things. She had been in this place of desire before. More than once, more than twice. Finding herself torn apart. Split into two, dismantled in despair. But she continued to remain optimistic, still soul searching for the man of her dreams.

Swallowing down the infatuation blockage, that swamped her throat with gullibility. She gently tapped into a conversation of life, loves and regrets. Her words misted by the aching pain of loneliness, softened the severity of her inquiry. She was looking for more than a rump, at present. More than a one night stand. As she endeavoured with enquiries. Each reply precise, exacting, warming the essence of her soul. The music sweet, soothing, capturing the spirit of how she felt. She became scared to make that initial eye contact. Afraid of its deep commitment. What it would say, mean. Afraid of her own weakness. Was she about to make a mistake!! Was he the man that would break the curse. The man that would dismantle the destructive element, that dwelt within. Had he reached a peek in life. Walking those sane steps. Was he looking to settle down? Does he know about love. Could he teach her what she needed to know, or was he a masquerade of a man that would know. Was she ready to give a romance, with him, a try. Their union too young, for her extremity. Only time would tell its end . . . .

Communication,
let's continue!!

The circulating space surrounding her, felt blithe, buoyant, open to persuasion. He sensed admiration. Desire of a kind. He felt anxiety bow its distorted head before her. Apprehension concealed itself, in his dry wit; instigating insecure logic. He introduced himself, not wanting to materialize pushy, or over eager. He sat beside her, keen to gain her trust and respect. Taken in by her innocence. Mesmerised by her physic. He found himself concentrating on nothing, but her rigorous breathing. He licked his lips in lust. Disguising the gesture, as an extended swallow of beer. Her heaving breasts took preference in his mind, obscuring her indigestible words. She spoke of many things. Complex things. Things that meant nothing, part from the accomplishment of his unconventional goal. Her hair glistened within the dim luminance. Her sun kissed complexion, paler under the blue fluoresce. The astound astonishment of her aura, consumed his aching heart; coherent in his soul. Her sonata voice delicately enchanted him, delivering a serene, secret message behind the effortless whispers. He gained a concept of her desires, her yearning; but it was hard for him to truly comprehend, through the ingenuous touch she gave.

He illicitly continued to gaze at her cleavage, ubiquitously rapt. In his mind, he wanted her nude. His thoughts insinuating impetuous requests, deafening her tiring vivid chat. He wanted to drag her from the establishment. Caress her neck. Affectionately entwine their bodies, gathering informational data, in that more appreciative way. But he perpetually listened to her witter about regrets, past relationships and prospects. He walked away; but soon found himself located by her side. Since noticing from a distance, pointed by his opinionated friends. Lifting his plausible interest. Gaining his perpetual recognition, was a depict exposure of lace panties. With the eyes of passion, firmly fixed, he became obsessed. Too thick skinned to be scared by her trivia. He showed interest. Agreeing, disagreeing, swapping ideas. Revelling in each others ideals. Spinning debates towards his favour. Eye contact was made. Was she an angel or a demon in disguise, created to mock poor gods and mankind. Was she here as a charade, chaos, arbitrary. His desire grew. The echoing thoughts of forbidden fruit enticed. No other would do, for that night. Could she convey his imagination. Lift his expectations! His tenure throbbed. Would she blow his mind; his socks away. How far would his toes curl? Could they go all the way! If she achieved the ultimate of these, he knew he would be hers for the rest of his life, and eternity. Desiring to be unfaithful; anymore . . . .

A
reasoning
kiss

With the nightspot concluding, the disc jockey implemented his final tune. Negligent of all thought, she seized his threads, hastening him outside. Abandoning company. Away from prying eyes. It was at a dormant time. The numinous time, between dusk and dawn, as the faltering shadows fought for supremacy, over the convictional emission of daybreak. Its sweet arousing essence, intertwined its miraculous officious impression. Mingling an authentic illusion within the mild breeze that cooled their sculptured features; flippantly communing a soothing symphony. Bathing its multi directional blast, through the twisting branches and leaves, of the subliminal tree tops; and stagnant bric-a-brac. Merrily: clinking, whistling its serene serenade. Issuing a unique construction, in the paranormal melody; specially composed by the amorous night sorcerers. Their tepid auras, isolating their physic, from the weary zombies that entered the desolate streets. Unstable, she grabbed hold of his arm; stabilising from the sudden surge of fresh air. While the rapturous song of stirring birds, summonsed tranquillity; towards its mystic sonnet. The rhythmical sound of her shoes, issued a separate dimension, within mother natures astounding, exceptional sound. She felt at ease. He was stupendous. Feelings of safety and security consumed, in his fervent grasp. She glanced up at his manly silhouette. Dashing and clear. Inapprehensive of her stagnate mind. She felt lucky being by his side.

Peace was their idiom, as they communed, listening to natures ulterior reverberation. Impression of ecstasy filled her soul. In her heart, she sensed the need to discover. How he tasted! How he felt! But emerged as a fool, powerless to converse her illicit intimate desire. She became a puppet for a twilight puppeteer. Incapable of controlling her suppressed emotions. Inept to curb the evolved episode, she unintentionally released the conceited attributes, that kept her safe from harm. Allowing a miraculous consenting moment; descend. Suffusing its inquisitive delight. She face him, as she incorporated her delicate hands on his chest. Her heart beating hard. She searched for acknowledgement in his vacant glance. Feeling no restriction, she lent forward. Slowly, their lips touched, warming the essence of her soul. She became lost in time. Lost in space. Uncertain whether it was the alcohol consumption, or softness of his embrace, allocating the momentary lose of balance. Baffled; she pulled herself away. Afraid of its elicit content. She wallowed in ore, becoming optimistic of the night. But her curious confidence dared not challenge the mystical fate; that night . . . .

A
kiss to
remember

The club condensed with ferment excitement, despite the fact it was coming to an end. As the final intimate dance was instrumented, at the cocktail bar, he was ordering the final round. Unconscious of the subsequent event. He found himself swayed from this desire. Split from the locality of his companions. Extracted from the barman's mortified rebuff. Shaken; his limbs became weak, by the unexpected innovation. Amazed; he induced no reason to disobey, her feminine intuition. Open minded he followed her blindly, unsure of her intent, but with one thing firmly in mind. Subtracted out of bustling excitement. Swayed into a cool vacant space, full of mystic charm. In his instability, he found he was submerged in unity, urbanized by alcohol consumption. Through intoxicated eyes, he became sheltered in sorcery; never perceiving a miraculous facilitated glow, in the crack of dawn. Was it her jovial friendship, or his endeavoured admiration! Uneasy: he had to break free. Devour the serene density, priming the air with love. But the style, fulfilling this objective, evaded his mind. He glanced at her for inspiration. His eyes fixating to one place. Secretly, he licked his lips, as he gazed at her protruding breasts. Her luxuriant skin, shimmered in extremity under the gentle street lamps. Close to the boundary of losing dignity, he achingly looked away, not wanting to break the sensuality of his esteem.

He felt the tendency to be near her. With her, touching her. They stopped. The moons reflective lustre, shone bright, casting a receptive ambient for the perfect stage. She turn to him ecstatic. His callous soul crumbled, from the incessant gaze within her eyes. His profound desire to kiss her, escalated; as his will to be her man. He yearned to utilize a ardent embrace, but his encroachment remained limited by her palms. Naïve within the instigated pursued passion in his forlorn heart. His soul coveted to be renewed. To be younger; unknown. A boy. A toddler without a clue. He became lost within his craving. Mislaid in his needs. Unable to decipher his scathing lust. A numinous, magical energy intervened, ascertaining the ration for their lips embrace. Their mouths parted, leaving a loving, delicate, imprint on his lips. An imprint of things that could come. An imprint of her desire. His head swirled under the impact of her sweet awe, giving him a lustful desire. He sought for more! He wanted to taste more. More of the sticky substance that oozed from the pores of her lips. The sweet essence of strawberries, complimenting her natural tang. But before he could make a decisive move, she walked away. Leaving him watch her being driven away . . . .

Collision
of
fate!!

Submerged in irrationality, the eternal taste of her tender kiss, haunted his mind. The delicate scent of her physic, echoed his thoughts. Her magnetic charm, her complexion; compelled his ego. The requisite innocents within the depths of her ellipse eyes, peered into the nadir of his hazed core. Stealing his thoughts. His heart. His soul. Dismantling the essence of his repetitive perfidy. His mind inspired. Optimistic of her call. He paced the corridors, constructing an assumed conversation. He gazed at the far-off receptor. His actions incisive; a lifestyle battle had commenced. Nine hours had passed!!

Conscious of her momentary weakness, her lapse of dignity. That brief kiss. The way she scampered, afraid of the embryonic moment. She hoped he'd call. She subdued the uncertainty of her uncharted desire. Her heart lustful, leaping at the cells mere sound. Nonsensical; upsetting, disturbing. An absurd end to what should of been! Losing contentment, ease. Awkwardness assumed. Despair triumphed, as the moment arrived. Handset jingled in the distant; sound strange to her ear. It rang once. Her heart pounded harder, deeper. It rang twice. Uncertainty gathered. Was it him? The deceptive tone jerked her progress. It rang for the third time, she answered.

Words escaped that silent moment of expectation. Doubt amassed in his heart, indistinguishable to hers. Her voice shaky, alluring, breaking the desolate void. Overwhelmed by beguilement, he replied. The fragmentation of space; stagnant, as they relaxed. She stoked her leg. He gained a wide smile. They spoke of many things. His first glance; reminiscing of the night, events. Mesmerised by truth, their desire to congregate merged. He felt the conquering yearn to be with her, by her. She wanted more. Out of the blue, an invite was cast. Shocked, grateful for the opportunity it was accepted.

The journey was long, as she succumbed to vagueness. He arose early, aspiring an impression. Time flew slow, but their anticipation escalated. She knocked on the door. Their eyes met. The atmosphere estranged by hesitance, against their brewing lust. Bending to convention of strangers, they greeted each other with insincerity, against the reality of their truth. As they escaped the populous, to privacy; intuition grasped hold. They re-enacted their greeting earnestly. Prolonging this intervention to the hour she had to go. It was indeed, the beginning, the beginning of a beautiful friendship . . . .

Printed in the United States
By Bookmasters